Auberon Herbert

Windfall and waterdrift

Auberon Herbert

Windfall and waterdrift

ISBN/EAN: 9783337141394

Printed in Europe, USA, Canada, Australia, Japan

Cover: Foto ©Andreas Hilbeck / pixelio.de

More available books at **www.hansebooks.com**

WINDFALL

AND

WATERDRIFT

BY

AUBERON HERBERT.

Williams & Norgate :

14, Henrietta Street, Covent Garden, London;
and 20, South Frederick Street, Edinburgh.

G. P. Putnam's Sons : New York.

———

1894.

To E. and E.,

Truest of true friends, I offer this little book,

—fruit of the hours spent in wanderings on

highway and by-way.

CONTENTS.

xii.

xiii.

WINDFALL & WATERDRIFT.

THE NEW COMRADE.

IF heart and tongue be true, be true,
  Would scorn to trick or trip,
If heart be gay through the toil of day,
  And jest be ready on lip ;

If hand and eye be quick to guard,
  And foot be slow to flee,—
Then fare with us, and share with us,
  Beneath the greenwood tree.

MY FEET ARE DRAWN.

" Oh ! Mother, Mother, soon your child
  No more your child will be,
For dusk and dawn my feet are drawn
  Towards the fairy lea.

" With out-stretched hand and flattering word
  The path is all beset ;
My heart is like a poor lost bird,
  That flutters in the net."

BROKEN BRIDGES.

" WE have lived too long by hill and glen,
   And another home we'll search ;
We'll make our peace with the King's proud
   men,
   And be sained by Holy Church.

" And we'll have no toil but to labour the soil,
   And watch the good corn grow ;
For every drop of blood that is shed,
   But brings its certain woe."

" Oh ! no, sweet maid, for Church and King,
   Are as false as false as Hell,—
The life we have led must its own end bring,
   And the end when it comes is well."

·BY THE CAMP-FIRE.

Good cheer,—beneath the great tall trees,
  With the camp-fire burning red,
As you lie and hear the creeping breeze
  In the green roof over-head.

Pile up the broken wood, sweet maid,
  And make the night yield room ;
For who shall say in forest glade,
  What strange things walk the gloom ?

YEA AND NAY.

FOR she said nay, and I said yea,
  And we parted with frown and tear ;
And I turned away on that very day,
  And lost my only dear.

Through the crowded street with downcast eyes
  She creeps from place to place ;
And when we meet, love's sweet surprise
  No more lights up her face.

THE GREAT WHITE WAVE.

" A GRACE, a grace, to-night I crave,—
    My heart it bodes me ill ;
  For oh ! I dreamt of a great white wave,
    And it grew greater still."

"There's never a need for thy poor heart's moan,—
    Let be, sweet wife, let be ;
  For a hundred times has the wild wind blown,
    And blown no hurt to me."

He touched her cheek with his touch so light,
    And her hands as if in play ;
  Then out he passed to the cruel night,
    That raged to seize its prey.

THE MIRROR AND THE SOUL.

Ah, my fair one, none to equal
　　Thee in beauty could there be ;
Yet I wonder of the sequel—
　　What that beauty did for thee ?

Was the self within thee fashioned,
　　Purer, nobler, than the rest ;
Was the soul itself impassioned
　　By the face we loved the best ?

THE HILLS ABOVE THE RIVER.

SHE crossed the plain beyond the wood,
　　Where the russet heath was growing,
Until she saw the hills that stood
　　Above the river flowing.

" Flow on, brave stream, with never a rest,
　　Till thou findest the open sea ;
There's a hunger to wander within my breast,
　　To wander and go with thee."

THE BITTER HOUR.

THE storm has leapt on the forest,
   Intent on its cruel end,
And the strife is at its sorest,
   As the great trees toss and bend.

But brother stands by brother,
   In that wild and bitter hour,
And each gives help to other,
   Against the mad fiend's power.

GROWING SHADOWS.

Shadowy grows the world around me,
  Things of joy and things of pain ;
Slowly fades their substance from them,
  Losing hold upon the brain.

Ghosts, they seem just flitting past me,
  Seen an hour but cannot stay,
Scarcely power to harm or help me,
  As I glide my downward way.

Only still the half-seen meanings,
  Souls of all these human things,
Keep their form and keep their power,
  Undisturbed, like spirit-kings.

WHAT LUCK——

WHAT luck shall be thine, small boat, to find,
   As thou sailest into the night?
Will the winds of the shore come tripping behind,
   To hasten thy merry flight ;

Will the stars be kind, and the laughing waves
   Just dimple the moonlit sea ;
Or thy foes leap out from the great cloud-caves,
   To challenge a dance with thee ?

"ONE MORE NOW."

WITH gloomy brows they sat at the board,
　For small the hope could be,
When the fair-haired lad with his wooden
　　sword,
　Strode up to his father's knee.

"Oh ! here is a hand, if you're all too few,
　Oh ! here is a sword for fight ;
And we've one more now, and there's little
　　to do,
　But to put yon foe to flight."

GAILY ONWARDS.

CARELESS of the hurt and slip,
   Heat of plain or mountain snow,
Trust in heart, and song on lip,
   Gaily onwards we two go.

Fret of life away we fling,
   As from hill to hill we climb ;
We shall make him laugh and sing
   All the way grey-bearded time.

OLD-TIME THINGS.

"Oh ! what have you done with the old-time
    things;—
  With our walk by the garden wall,
And the listening look, where the faint smile
    clings,
  And the words, which were sweeter than all?

"Are they lost and gone? Have you thrown them
    by,
  As things too light to keep ;
Or is there a nook where they're suffered to lie,
  And wake for a while from their sleep?

" For oh ! in my heart 'tis as yesterday,—
  And the years can't make it far,
But they're ever with me, as a breath of the sea,
  To gladden the days that are."

IS IT WORTH YOUR WHILE FOR THIS?

" If I am to love,—if so I must,—
　　I this perhaps might do,—
　I could stamp my heart to the smallest dust,
　　And hide it away from you !

" You could have, if you chose, as in trance a
　　bride,
　　With lips that are white to kiss,
　And the touch of her hands as of one who has
　　died—
　　Is it worth your while for this ? "

EYES THAT FLINCH NOT.

And if you cross him as you go,—
  And many a form has he ;
To some he's pain, or shame, or woe,
  Or death itself, may be ;

You'll look him in the face with eyes,
  That flinch not his to meet,
Until the bitterest shaft, that flies,
  Falls harmless at your feet.

"OH! MUCH WOULD I GIVE."

" Oh ! Laddie, bid me rise and come,
    To travel afield with thee ;
I'll walk thy road and carry thy load,
    And weary I'll never be."

" Now cease, little girl, and hold your peace ;
    You must stay to sew and to spin ;
For how can you travel the world with me,
    Where lives are to lose and win ? "

He's lying stricken on burning sand,
    Where grows the tall palm-tree :—
" Oh ! much would I give for that little hand,
    To staunch the blood for me."

THE YEARS ARE NOUGHT.

In wonder spoke those sweet, sweet lips—
How many a year ago !—
As she named the name of a stranger boy,
In a cadence soft and low.

She has forgotten the passing thought,
Forgotten the passing name ;
But to me the years are nought, are nought,
And the sweet voice sounds the same.

"AND NOW MY LOVING IS DONE."

" OH ! turn, oh ! turn your horse's head,
    And ride again with me."
" I'll not draw rein, or turn again,
    Until I reach the sea."

" For your heart is light as a mocking-bird,
    That never could be won ;
    It is nought that the love of the years has
        brought,
    And now my loving is done."

CHANGED TIMES.

THEN up and spoke the bright-eyed bird,
Red Robin—it was he :—
" Oh is it true the news I've heard,—
There's one to marry thee ?

" No more I'll haunt your sunny lawn,
The dainty bread to take ;
Or sing anear your bed at morn
My carol for your sake.

" So fare you well—tis sore to part,
And yet the thing must be,—
You've taken another love to your heart,
And left no place for me."

WITH THE MEASURE THAT YOU MEASURE——

" I HAVE done a cruel thing," she cried,
   " I have stricken a heart with pain ;
I have cast the old, old love aside,
   And broken the bond in twain.

" But wrong, perchance, begets its wrong,—
   And how, sweet love, shall it be,
In the years so far, in the years so long,
   If you are as false to me ? "

FAR AWAY IN ROSELAND.

OH ! far away in Roseland
  Is a cottage known to me,
And the breezes blow about it,
  From off the sunlit sea.

And a maiden sits and watches
  At sunset and sunrise,
And draws to herself the beauty
  Of waves and changing skies.

A WORD.

OH ! there is a word that lightens it all,
  The trial and toil of the day,
That helps us through, whatever befall,—
  But a word that is hard to say !

It comes to our lips, and we lose it again,
  In the midst of the world's wild fray ;
But oh ! it would soften the strifes of men,—
  That word, which is hard to say !

JOHN SMITH'S PHOTOGRAPH.

LINE upon line, it was graven there,—
  The tender heart, and the courage true,
The dreamer's dream of the futures fair,
  The will, that could win its passage through.

Yet he failed, you say, did nothing,—'twas hard;
  And you stand for a while, and wonder why
The Master Potter should labour a shard,
  Then fling it aside, and let it lie.

IN A SHORT HALF HOUR.

"Ah! love, we may look it straight in the face,—
No force could stem the flow ;
And it soon must pass,—our time of grace,
In a short half hour or so.

" We need not grieve ; we have loved too well;
There is nothing we care to undo ;
And never a word to break love's spell
Was spoken betwixt us two.

" But perhaps, perhaps, there is loss with the gain,
When lives so closely touch ;
And 'tis hardly meant in this world of pain,
That hearts should love too much."

A SECRET OF NATURE.

THERE'S a youth who leans at a window,
  And looks o'er sea and sky,
And his soul is filled with sweetness,—
  'Twere hardly pain to die.

There's a maid who leans at a window,
  No lover or loved one is nigh,
And her heart is drawn from her bosom,—
  But she could not tell you why.

THE TWO HEARTS.

"Oh mine," he said, "is the wanderer's heart,
  That glanceth from spray to spray,
That loveth here, that loveth there,
  And changeth every day ;
And such as it is, 'tis yours to take,
  And to keep, if so you may."

"Oh mine," she said, " is the heart that loves,
  But once with a perfect trust ;
That never can change, but still loves on,
  Till all things turn to dust ;
And such as it is, 'tis yours to take,
  To have and to hurt, if you must."

LET IT CARRY IT JUST WHERE IT WILL!

AND I said,—"Let it carry our little boat
  On its waters strong and still ;
And on and on, till the day breaks wan—
  Let it carry it just where it will.

" We shall glide by the shallows that flash in the
    light,
  By the pools where the deep weeds drown,
By the sloping lawns, till it comes into sight,—
  The glare of the mighty town."

A YOUNG DANE IN 1864.

" It might have struck another—that shell,
 Not him, so young and fair ;
There were plenty of us who had served as
 well,—
 And little to say or care.

" For he was a joy and a light to us all,
 With his laugh and his merry eye ;
And he is the one who is first to fall,—
 Not useless you or I."

"AN ASKING, GRANT YOU ME!"

" WILL you walk for a while in the garden fair,
    Where the soft winds move with a sigh ;
  Will you linger a while in the deep wood there,
    Where the lights with the shadows lie ;

" From the wood to the plain, and the plain to the
      wood,
    Will you follow the distant sky ;
  Will you wander away and away for good,
      Until the day we die ? "

UNSEEN BY THY SIDE.

" Few, few, my words—'tis short the grace—
   And minutes pass so swift ;
We may no more talk face to face,
   Or seek the veil to lift.

" Yet often by thy side I'll stand—
   Thou wilt not hear or see—
And strive to share in pain and care,
   And take a part from thee."

IF EVER——

" THY race, and thy land, and its sky above,
  All thine, mine too shall be ;
I will look no more in the faces I love,
  But rise and go with thee.

" And one thing, one, thou shalt promise
      and do,
  If thy love should weary of me,—
Thou shalt drive thy knife to my heart right
      through,
  Or ever I know and see."

A SHADOW THAT CROSSES THE SEA.

WE can almost laugh, at the mocking part,
  That fell for a while to us twain,
Though the tears of blood rose up in the heart,
  And dropped in their bitter rain.

For it seems so small, it can hardly count,
  In the course of the things to be,
Just a grain out of place in the long life-amount,
  Just a shadow that crosses the sea.

WHAT WOULD YOU SAY?

" We have finished our journey of many miles,
  With hearts that were true, old friend,
  With days of tears and with days of smiles,
  And now we are close to the end.

" There was many a toil, and many a slip,
  And many a day's wild weather ;
  But we closed our hands in a firmer grip,
  And our hearts beat truer together.

" But what would you say, if one should ask,
  As we stand here close at the end :—
' Would you live it again, as you lived it then ?'—
  Oh ! what would you say, old friend ? "

CLEFT IN TWAIN.

In the west is the golden glory,
  As the great king goes to his rest ;
In the east the purple staineth
  The hills from foot to crest.

And I stand and look in wonder,
  Till my heart is cleft in twain,—
Half for the vision of glory,
  And half for the dying pain.

NEVER A TIME FOR SITTING & SIGHING.

OH ! to tread the mountain land,
  Feel the world before one,
Pack on back and stick in hand,—
  Never a care comes o'er one.

Hour by hour the sweet day flying,
  Mountains open, valleys close,
Life with hundred voices crying,
  While the young blood strongly flows.

SO FAR.

So far, so far, as it can go,
My heart goes roving away,
While I sit alone and the shadows grow,
Close round where the red flames play ;

To the nestling valley that opens and dips,
To the snow-touched hills that gleam,
To the great seas hushed at the foot of their
cliffs,
That lie so still and dream.

A BUTTERFLY'S HEART.

" Your love, sweet sir, you had better save,
  Till the end of time may be,
Or cast it abroad on wind and wave,
  Than give it in charge to me.

" For this heart of mine is the lightest thing,
  That ever breath did blow,
Just a butterfly's heart to dance and to sing,
  As its fancies come and go."

THE ROSE AND THE LION.

"OH! you have been nurtured in soft smooth ways,
  Where the rough wind never blows,
  And the air is hushed through the golden days,
  And sweet with the scent of the rose.

" And I am rude, as the wave is rude,
  When the storms on the great sea beat,
  But mine is the will, and the conquering mood,
  That can place the world at your feet."

DIDST LAUGH OR CRY?

"Oh ! poor torn hulk in Love's wild game,
  Worn out, left almost dry,
When that young boy told all his flame,
  Oh ! didst thou laugh or cry?

" Didst laugh for sake of such last gain,
  Or cry, because that heart,
The world had not had time to stain,
  Would soon be what thou art? "

THE TWO FAR-OFFS.

FORWARD we look and we gild it all,
  Rich is the picture and tender and fair ;
Backward we look and the blue mists fall,
  Veiling the troubles that once were there.

Ah ! well and ah ! well, and lighter the load,
  If heart the enchanter weaves his web ;
If he tells love-stories to cheat the road,
  And binds in our dreams his purple thread.

THE SHADOWLESS FACE.

"Oh! well, for him the path who tries,
  If that his soul endure,
 If he may meet the stern dread eyes,
  With constant will and sure.

"But woe—take heed—before I call,
  If that thy cheek grow pale,
 At clutch of fear, or eyes should fall,
  And heart and purpose fail."

Then came the face; as if I dreamed,—
  No shadow, and no sound;
 It hung, and gazed on me, and seemed
  To crush me to the ground.

That face!—I count long hours, long days,—
  It beats upon mine eyes;
 And still my soul thrusts back its gaze,
  Until the dread thing dies.

FOR ONE SHORT DAY.

Love me, love, for one short day,—
   That is all I ask of you ;
You may send me then away,
   And your happy path pursue.

Would you grant the thing I crave—
   Tender word and heart's caress—
You'd not miss the gift you gave,
   Love's sweet store would not be less.

Would you smile and say me yea,—
   Loan of heart this while to lend,—
It would last me all the way,
   Till I reach my Journey's end.

MORE THAN THE REST.

A MILE or two and a mile away,
  And there, old sea, thou art ;
And with each new day I walk to the bay,
  To gladden and quicken my heart.

Oh ! great world-soul with thy mighty tides,
  Thou art more than all the rest,
With thy soft child's play and thy tender way,
  And the passion deep in thy breast.

ALL HAD BEEN WELL.

"Oh ! love, my love—but there was the loss—
  All had been well, had we but held hands ;
The hill to climb, and the sea to cross,
  And the strange wild life in the strange new
    lands.

"All had been well—we had laughed at the toil,
  At the faults and mishaps that the morrow
    would mend,
Met the smooth with the rough, whilst the light
    was enough,
  Then slept on together when all was at end."

THEY TAKE NO HEED.

"Oh ! whether I'm dead I hardly know—
  Whatever dead may be—
But they make no space, and they keep no place,
  And take no heed of me.

"I creep and I stand, and I touch their hand,
  As they speak to each other there ;
But the words that I say they can't understand,
  And they fall on the empty air."

THE HUMAN SKEIN.

THE far lights gleam across the bay,—
    They hold my soul in trance,
For they tell of life with its grave and gay,
    And its strangely mixed romance.

Each star-point there means home and love,
    And strife and sorrow and pain,—
The threads from below, and the threads from above,
    That mix in the human skein.

AN OLD FRIEND.

I HAVE waited, old friend, for your last command,
  And now has come the day,
When we both understand we must take in hand
  A bout of good sword play.

I shall hold my guard and look in your face,
  And am ready the worst to endure ;
And though you must win, I shall ask no grace,
  From your strokes so keen and sure.

RESTLESS AND USELESS.

FOR to-night my heart is a poor lost thing,
  With a restless useless pain,
And the pitying skies no comfort bring,—
  Their tender touch is in vain.

And I do not know what the pain may be,
  But this one thing alone,—
That the heart must ache like the troubled sea,
  In wayward moods of its own.

50

ON THE GREAT WASTE HEAP.*

AND still she asked, as she sat and leant,
Leaning and dreaming half-asleep,
Were they only fit, the years she had spent,
Just to be thrown on the great waste-heap?

In the desert behind, of the things she has done,
Which of them all was worth its pain ;
In the desert in front, what good can be won
From the purposeless years that still remain?

*NOTE.—See a critique in the *Speaker* (by G. M. ?) on
Whistler's picture of a lady before a mirror.   I do not
remember the date.—A. H.

MY FINGERS, NOT MY HEART.

My fingers traced the word, 'tis true,
  My fingers, not my heart;
In all the wrong they did to you,
  It never took its part.

They pressed on me, like hunted thing,
  That's caught in mesh and line ;
'Twas they, not I, who spoke the lie,
  And still the heart is thine.

A LOST GIFT.

IT is hard to believe that such things be,—
    You may take it for what it is worth ;
For she that came and talked to me,
    Was not of the race of earth.

But I stained my soul, as 'tis easy to see,
    With the touch of the common clay ;
And the earth and the sky grew empty for me,
    And their gift was taken away.

A BROKEN THREAD.

THAT silence—yes ! 'twas yours not mine,
   You dropt my hand that day ;
The long months passed,—you made no sign,
   And found no word to say.

And yet I dream'd you stood last night,
   In your old pleasant way,
And talked of all the trifles light,
   And what the gossips say.

Your kind good self, that once I knew—
   But that's no longer so—
Well, well—how fares it now with you,
   As on the swift years go ?

A STRANGE NEW HEART.

" AND what did I do with my heart, you ask ?—
Oh ! never to pause and never to think,
But hide it away from myself,—was my task,
And guard my feet from nearing the brink.

" And slowly I made from the needful stuff
A strange new heart that served as my own,
That laughed and talked and was good enough,—
Except, may be, in the night alone.

" But can I return, now it all is o'er,—
So far away from myself I have strayed,—
To the thing that I was in the days before
This strange new heart for myself I made ?"

WHEN THE DEAD ARE STANDING BY.

'TWAS a small bright home,—those three, his
    wife,
  Poor Jack, and his well-tried friend ;
But the flesh is weak in the daily strife,
  And the Devil looks to the end.

So it came to pass through slip and slip
  That friend and wife were untrue ;
And they lied to Jack, till the day he died,
  With his constant trust in the two.

And now they are free to enjoy their bliss,—
  But perchance were it you or I,
We might shudder and turn from the sweet
    love-kiss,
  When the dead were standing by.

WOULD YOU TAKE OR PASS THE CUP?

Oh ! the days, the days so golden,
   Bright as rivers in their flow,—
Strength, so proud and unbeholden,
   In the days of long ago !

Now the brain is cold and joyless,
   And the pulse beats very slow,
And the empty days are toilless,—
   So unlike the long ago !

Gone, the fire, the joy, the pride,
   Gone, the spirits' rush and flow,
Gone, the life-blood's surging tide,—
   Gone with days of long ago.

Yet, and if they brought you waters,
   Magic waters to drink up,—
Youth again, renewed as then—
   Would you take or pass the cup?

GREATER THAN EVER WOULD BE.

For the world that night had a beauty,
  Greater than ever could be,
As the moon in its silent passion
  Hung trembling over the sea.

But my heart still kept a misgiving,
  And whispered of sorrow to be—
That the clouds would come stealing between us,
  To trouble my dream and me.

THE MADMAN'S PLAY.

For oh ! the house is an evil house,
  Where strange things have their way,
And when all is at rest but the scampering mouse,
  Begins the madman's play.

For a breath is blown as you walk alone,
  And the candle flickers out ;
And they pluck at your dress with a laugh or
  groan,—
Then away in their rabble rout.

A SOUL BORN AGAIN.

For ah ! those changes of soul, my friend,
  That are born by a special grace,
When the old life comes to its sudden end,
  And the new slips into its place.

To the hall of pictures he idly went—
  Just one of the idlers he—
And little to him their language meant,
  For his soul was dead to see.

When a woman and child—do you know it there?—
  With a sad far look in her face,
Just fixed his listless wandering stare,
  And held him fast to his place.

And the while he looked, a new world rose,
  From which he had lived apart,
And a strange soft light grew out of the night,
  And dawned on his careless heart.

THAT NEVER I LOSE HIM MORE.

" Oh ! who are you on this stormy night,
  And how shall I render you aid,
For your hands are all too fine and white
  For the hands of a beggar-maid ? "

" Oh ! little am I but a beggar-maid,
  And I pray to rest my head,
Where your dog and your horse in the stall are
    laid,
  With a crust of your broken bread."

" And why are you here on the wide world tost,
  And why have you wandered away ? "
" I wander to find the love I have lost,
  This many and many a day.

" For once my heart was a light, light heart,—
  Oh ! light as a wave of the sea,—
So he left me to play my mocking part,
  And went on his way from me.

"And many's the town I have wandered through,
  And hill and valley I've crost,
And often am wet with the cold night dew,
  In search of the love I have lost ;

"And I wander on till the stars above
  Shall guide my feet to his door ;
And then I shall bind him in arms of love,
  That never I lose him more."

YOU TOO !

" So you too stooped to the common dust,—
    The commonest dust men tread ;
  You whom I knew with the frank clear eyes,
    And the fearless poise of the head !

"Oh ! strange, that the hand, so strong to save,
    Should shatter my good and true ;
  That you who lifted me out of the grave,
    Your own soul's work should undo."

BY THE UNKNOWN WAY.

I HAVE said goodbye to the friends of my race,—
The greetings are over and done,—
And I journey forth to find me a place
To take last leave of the sun.

For I never could die where the four walls stand,
And hide the sun from me,
But the sky must be bare on either hand,
With the great air moving free.

And dimmer and dimmer will grow the light,
As the pulses cease their play,
Till the soul speeds forth on its homeward flight,
Far off, by the unknown way.

WHERE THE FAR LIGHTS BURNT.

Ah ! love, so sweet and patient and fond,
  I wandered far from thy sight,
For I said to myself that the world beyond
  Was a garden of rich delight.

And there rose an image from morn to morn
  Of new bewildering days,
Till my heart grew proud, and I thought with scorn
  Of the peaceful homely ways.

For the young are light, and I never had learnt
  To know the false from the true,
And my feet were drawn where the far lights burnt
  With their wonder strange and new.

And now how bitter to heart is the taste,
  And gone are the folly and pride,
And I save what I can from the years of waste,
  And stand once more at thy side.

OH! THIN THE LINE.

" SAY, master, say, how men shall learn
The hidden truths to speak,
To feed the inward fires that burn,
The far-off knowledge seek."

" If ye would win the gift within,—
So toil for many a day,—
And yet, forsooth, the truest truth
May come by other way.

" Oh ! thin the line this world that parts
From other worlds, be sure ;
And strange things drop within the hearts,—
The open hearts and pure."

THE TWO BRIDALS.

The bridal was fixed for the coming day,
 And they feasted late and deep ;
But the bride she tossed on her bed as she lay,—
 That night she could win no sleep.

She sees a face as there she lies,
 And oh ! its eyes are sad,—
Those honest laughing good brown eyes,
 That never sadness had.

Then rose a voice that sang its song,
 And soft it sang and low :—
" Oh ! better it were in the greenwood there,
 If you and I should go ;

" Oh ! better it were by bracken and bush,
 Than in castle and castle hall,
And to wander at will o'er plain and hill,
 And among the good trees tall ;

"And better the breath of the woodland air,
    That is sweet as honey to lip,
And to loiter and stray through the summer day,
    Till the sun begins to dip ;

"And the fire at night, that flings its light
    On the tall stems wan and bare,
When the shadows press near, but shrink in fear,
    Like ghosts, from the ruddy glare ;

" And better to wed in the mystic glade,
    Where the dawn comes creeping through,
And the fern is laid, and the bed is made,
    Amongst the oak and the yew ;

" For the others shall wed in silken dress
    And in holy church,—who will ;
But we will wed with the trees o'erhead,
    When the birds are hushed and still.

" Then leave it all, and come with me—
  My forest-rose to bloom—
And the bridal shall be in the great woods free,
  Where the green leaves clothe the room."

Then forth she leant and sang her song,—
  So soft in the air and low :—
"Far better it were in the greenwood there,
  If you and I should go.

" My soul is sick of their dainty things—
  For others their gifts shall be—
They have brought me all that the red gold
    brings,
  But never a heart for me.

" Oh ! better to wed where the great trees old
  Shall sing in the wind o'erhead,
Than to starve in the midst of their silk and gold,
  When the heart within is dead."

NOT WORTH MUCH ——

It wasn't worth much, as we understand,—
  The heart of a wild rash boy;
And it wasn't worth while to stretch your hand,
  To trifle with such a toy.

Ah me ! that heart has been lost and given,
  Oh ! many a day since then ;
But 'twill never be given on this side Heaven,
  In the same true way again.

THE LOVES THAT LOVE THE BROAD LANDS.

"Oh! mother, why do you urge me still,
  To make my poor heart grieve,
For I have a bride in the fairy hill,
  And her I cannot leave?

" And these others of yours, who are far above—
  Oh! small is their count of me,
For they think it a sin to give their love,
  Except where the broad lands be.

" But she loves not so, for her heart within
  Is truer than gold can be,
And she only cares my love to win,
  And return it in love to me."

WITH THE ROSES.

" For you in your home, true love, shall stay,
  ' Where never the rough winds blow,
  And the roses that gladden the summer day,
  In your own sweet fashion grow.

" And I'll come back from the storm and the strife,
  And never again will stray ;
  And we'll live with the roses, living their life,
  That grow in your own sweet way."

THE SEA BENEATH THE HILLS.

Yes! I shall go, and you will dream,
  And drink the pale blue sky,
Beneath the hills that hap you round,
  As silver days go by.

When others come your love to claim,
  You still, you pale, blue sea,
Oh! shall you mean for them the same,
  That once you meant for me ;

And shall they look on you with eyes
  As tender-true as mine,
And love each changing gleam that flies
  Across that face of thine ?

THE TWO WORLDS.

" You have called me twice, you have called me
thrice,
And what do you want with me ?
For the world of the living, the world of the
dead,
The same can never be ! "

" I have called you twice, I have called you thrice,
And without you I cannot be ;
For the world of the dead is my world of life,
And the living are dead to me."

FAR OUT ON THE COLD BLUE SEA.

" Now let your hand in mine be set,
　　And make me a promise true,—
　　If ever your heart should learn to forget,
　　This thing for me you'll do,—

" You'll row me out in yon small boat,
　　Far out on the cold blue sea ;
　　And you'll leave me there on the waves afloat,
　　To make their sport of me."

THROUGH IT ALL.

I COULD not love, and I could not trust,
  And I turned in my pride away,
And oh ! I would humble myself in the dust,
  If I might call back that day.

For I saw in his eyes the bitter pain, —
  ·" Let it be, let it be, as you will ; "
And the words, they burn to this day in my brain, —
  " Through it all, I shall love you still."

ITS HEART IS STIRRED.

SHE sang,—" I'm like a poor caged bird,
   That hangs against the wall,
And all day long its heart is stirred,
   To hear it's woodmates call.

   " Alas ! no love its wild heart stills,—
   It dreams of woodlands free,—
So I would wander on the hills,
   And sail the enchanted sea."

THEN AND NOW.

" I LOVED you then, and I sinned for you then,
   And the love was more than the sin ;
But the past is the past, and never again—
   For the love is dead within.

" It saved my soul, that sin of old,—
   There's nothing I could recall ;
But to sin again, when the heart is cold,
   Were the deadliest sin of all."

LIKE THE KING'S OWN SON.

I LOVED that boy, in his tasty dress,
  With a riband or two made gay ;
And I'd see him wait each day at the gate,
  As I passed on my homeward way.

He'd ride the horses when work was done,
  And oh ! it was fine to see !—
Perched up on his seat, like the King's own son,
  In the way of a King rode he !

One morning I missed that bright wee face,
  I've seen it no more since then ;
And oh ! in my heart is a hidden place,
  Which bleeds just now and again.

THE BREAD ON THE WATERS.

Ah ! yes, the loving dead they stand,
And stretch their hands to you ;
And as you pass to that far land,
Their loves your life renew ;

Sweet gifts of love your steps pursue ;
You gather what you sowed ;
You lived for love ; love waits for you,
In old or new abode.

NO TRUER COMRADE.

WITH our lives in our hands from morn to morn,
  She watched and toiled with me,
Till the scabbard grew thin and sorely worn,
  And the blade flashed bare and free.

I buried her there in the desert space,—
  No truer comrade than she,
To smile at the storm, and the worst to face,
  Whatever the worst might be.

A CRUEL WORD.

" You might have taken the molten lead,
　　And poured it on my breast ;
Or the naked sword which hangs by your bed—
　　Whichever had pleased you best ;

"And I would have kissed your hand, nor stirred,
　　And I would have bowed the head,—
But oh ! you have spoken a cruel word—
　　Hurts more than steel or lead.

" So I leave your home,—for I may not stay,
　　If my love is all too light—
And I'll break no more your bread by day,
　　Or sleep at your side by night."

A LINE OF SHADOW.

THE sea is at rest—for the storms are o'er—
  Just touched with the hand of night ;
And a line of shadow creeps to the shore,
  Then flashes in silver light,—

Like a note that stoops in its flight, and droops,
  And clings for a while to the ground ;
Then trembles and wakes from its trance and breaks
  Into passion and glory of sound.

ON THE FURTHER SIDE.

ONLY a bit of land-locked bay,
  With a haunting face on the further side ;
Yet the ocean as well might bar the way,
  So far from each other our lives divide.

For you jest at times, and at times you pray,
  And you tread a path that cannot be mine ;
And the world is with you from day to day,
  And all that you are, I dare not divine.

ALL RIGHT IN THE DOG'S HOLE.

LET them say what they will, 'tis little we care,—
　　We laugh to each other and wink,
For we know how to settle our own affair,
　　Whatever the wise ones think.

They turn up the white of their eyes to the sky,
　　With their mixture of pity and blame,
Yet our dog's-hole's all right by day and by night,
　　And our trust in each other the same.

RHYMES LEARNT LONG AGO.

" AYE, rough, sir, rough, for she'd often leak,—
  Rough life on those far-off seas ;
And never a one who cared to speak
  On dainty things like these.

" For to tell you the truth what helped me then,
  Was rhymes learnt long ago ;
And I'd say them over and over again,
  When the worst of the winds did blow.

" Just broken bits,—of a maiden fair
  As she stood in the summer light,—
But they gave me the heart to do and to bear
  On many a stormy night."*

*NOTE.—See a story told by Mr. Montefiore in the *Times*, after Lord Tennyson's death, of a sailor who knew by heart and used to repeat to himself much of Lord Tennyson's poetry.

THREE SHORT YEARS.

" THY hands are slipping, they hold so light,—
 Oh ! stay the hour with me ;
 I've thirsted so through day and night
 For sight and touch of thee."

" Let go, dear heart, I may not stay,—
 The power is ebbing fast ;
 But love me still from day to day,
 Till three short years are past.

" Then shall it end, the pain, the loss,—
 To thee my hands I'll reach ;
 And lightly thou shalt step across,
 And each belong to each."

MORNING AND EVENING.

In the glory of youth the young man went,—
  His heart with pride was stirred ;
" They should yield," he cried, " to the message
    sent,
  And force of the burning word."

The long years past, and a wearied man
  Crept back to the old home-door :—
" I have spoken my word, and none has heard,
  And the great world rolls as before."

NO TEARS ARE THERE.

SHE cannot weep—the springs are dry—
  No tears the eye-lids hold ;
She cannot feel—all feelings die,
  And soul lies dead and cold.

Some day perchance the spell may break,—
  When long still years are o'er,
From out the dust her heart may wake
  To feel and grieve once more.

THE BREAD OF TRUTH OR LIES.

HE stood in my dream, and he pressed me sore,
As he looked with his strong stern eyes :—
" When you broke your bread, as they cried to be
fed,
Was it bread of truth or lies ?

" Oh ! was it the best of your heart and brain,—
A sacrament bread that you gave ;
And the net that you spread for their souls—was
it set
To gather, to keep, and to save ;

"Or was it yourself, and the world, and it's worth—
For these did you turn from the true ? "—
" Dear master, I was but a worm of the earth,
And I did what the other worms do."

THE SHADOWS ARE LIFTED.

For the hurrying years were flying fast,
  And her image was dim to me,
And the shadows, they lay so thick on the past,
  It had almost ceased to be.

With her pleading look in her eyes to-night,
  She came and she stood by me ;
And the years and the shadows that darkened my
    sight
  In that moment ceased to be.

THE CRY THAT GOES BEFORE TROUBLE.

" I WARNED you twice and then again,
    But heed ye would not pay—
'Tis hard to reach is the heart of men,
    As they go on their daily way.

" Your father and fathers of old I warned,—
    Oh ! each in turn the same ;
But they laughed in their hearts and my cry
    they scorned,
    And to each the sorrow came.

BENEATH THE SURFACE.

THE curtains are drawn, and the talk goes on,
  Where the lamp its warm glow flings,
And they sit and speak with their faces wan
  Of the world and its lightest things.

But their eyes never meet in midst of their speech,
  For they know, as they talk, full well,
That a fire burns low in the heart of each,
  With the pain of a stifled hell.

WAITING TO JOG.

It's all up now with the poor old dog,—
    He's fought and finished his day ;
And he's tired and worn and waiting to jog
    In peace on his homeward way.

He carries his faults and his sins on his head—
    As thou must do with thine—
And he's ready to pay on the settling day,
    Whatever the Judge may assign.

MY HEART'S FIRST CHOICE.

" Just seen, just known, when we both were young,
    Yet bound by a strange heart-bond,
I shall find him at once the crowd among,
    In that great new world beyond.

" So young he was, when the rose-bloom failed,
    And the ring in his laughing voice,—
But the long long years have never availed
    To alter my heart's first choice."

THE VOID.

She stretches hands to midnight skies—
So vast, so void, they seem ;
And back unanswered come her cries,
And all is as a dream.

" Oh ! where art thou"—the far stars yield
No word to hopes or fears ;
From all that vast unmeasured field
No answering sign appears.

OH WHY DID YOU SLEEP?

SHE glided in, and stood by his bed,
  And gently the air was stirred :—
" Oh why did you sleep so deep," she said,
  " That my cry you never heard ?

" I called on the heart, I called on the hand,
  So ready to do and dare,
But the wind sped by, and laughed at my cry,
  And flung it abroad on the air.

" Then sleep on now till the hour to wake,
  And break no rest for me ;
To-morrow to grieve for your lost love's sake,—
  Oh ! time enough will be."

THE DAYS OF OLD BONDS.

THE hours and days and months all fly,—
   Each brings it's own things new;
They work their changeful will—but I
   No nearer am to you.

And yet some subtle bonds still hold,—
   And oh! are hard to break—
That were woven once in the days of old
   For many a sweet thing's sake.

AN OLD COMRADE COMES TO HIS END.

" For once we've been caught in bad weather,
　　But little the odds it makes ;
We've had many good days together,
　　And cheated friend death of the stakes.

" There's one thing—the little girl yonder—
　　You must kiss her, and take her apart,
And tell her I ever grew fonder—
　　It will go, like a knife, to her heart.

" These women—it's not easy mended—
　　They never the chances can learn ;
And they think that the world is just ended,
　　When the bad luck comes to their turn.

" Bad luck !—it is easy to make it—
    It once nearly cost me the game,
  With the thought of how she would take it,
    Whenever the straight shot came.

" She's just like the others, my Polly,—
    All plain sense she's somehow above,—
  And she never finds out 'tis a folly,
    To pour out, like water, her love.

" Now heave me bit straighter, and leave me—
    There's nothing to do could you stay ;
  They have drilled me the hole too neatly,
    And the blood is just trickling away."

THE WIND IS THE WIND.

Thou hast been but thy self, — thou hast not
   sinned,
  And there is no blame for thee ;
For the wave is the wave, and the wind is the wind,
  And the heart as the heart must be.

And never a bond was woven yet
  Could bind thy flight for a day ;
Thou must gather and take, or flit and forsake,
  Thou must wander at will or stay.

THE SWORD IN THE SKY.

" THE lines are crossed,—'tis hard to know,
 But this at least I see—
Bright hopes shall kindle, strife shall flow,
 And hearts shall ache for thee ;

" And sorrow for thyself and pain,—
 Oh ! duly shalt thou reap,—
And rash bold acts with hurt and stain,
 Till comes the last long sleep."

A LOOK AND A SMILE.

" Art weary lad," the old man said,
    " Has't travell'd a hundred mile ?
Nay, come within and break our bread,
    And rest thy heart the while."

" Oh ! I'll not tarry, or come within,
    For what is a hundred mile,
If I see my sweet love pass, and win
    But a look and a bonnie smile ?

IN THE STORM TOGETHER.

THERE are memories that shall bind us,—
  As we both have loved to tell,—
How we faced that day together,
  When the storm upon us fell ;

How you stood at post of danger,
  With clear eyes and fearless heart ;
How I touched your hand and whispered—
  " 'Twas right well you played your part."

THE PROCESSION OF THE ATOMS.

AND still the long white hours of night,
  Will thread their silent way,
And the lighted street, where strange hearts beat,
  Will gleam across the bay ;

And still the wave will kiss the rock,
  Beneath the midnight spell ;
Alone, my heart will find no part
  In all it loved so well.

FOR THE SWEET DAY'S SAKE.

Oh ! take me safe to your arms at last,—
  I've lived through the bitter worst ;
And the pain and the shame and the wrong are
    past,
  That hurt like hunger and thirst.

I bore it, love, though my heart should break,
  With my foot against the wall,
Through the long long years, for the sweet day's
    sake,
  That to-day shall mend it all.

THE HANDS ON THE DIAL.

" For better 'twere spilt and wasted,
  When thin and poor is the wine ;
And better were love untasted,
  From this worn heart of mine.

" Can the joys come back that are over,
  Can the pulses beat as before,
Can the world grow young, and recover
  The gladness that once it wore ?"

WHICH OF THE TWAIN?

AND which of the twain is the wiser,
  And which is the toiler in vain ;
Is it he who has conquered all knowledge
  With the force of his tireless brain ;

Or she, to whom earthly possessions
  Are shadows that pass and seem ;—
Is it she, who knows only her Heaven,
  Or he, who holds it a dream ?

LIKE SHIPS AT SEA.

For hearts are like the ships at sea,
And some sail fine and brave ;
And some are driven by winds of heaven,
And tossed from wave to wave.

And oh ! to think through storm and dark,
With hope grown chill within,
And the hungry reef the wave beneath,—
How sore the way to win !

THE BLOOD OF THE WANDERERS.

" To wander and wander while life remains,
　　And never to find me a place of rest,—
For the blood of the race flows through my veins
　　That wandered away to the unknown west.

" They wandered and wandered, and so will I,
　　Reaching and touching the world's far ends,
With the hill and the plain, the wind and the rain,
　　The sun and the stars, as their earthly friends.

" When the years are gone and strength is
　　　outworn,
　　And never a crust the good chance sends,
I shall curl me to sleep where the grasses grow
　　　deep,
　　And say goodbye to the old-time friends."

MIGHT HAVE BEEN.

Had we fixed it then beyond release,
  I might have lowered and coarsened your life,
Have dimmed its glory and troubled its peace,
  As you walked with me in the ways of strife ;

Or you might have braved the thing, and saved
  The lamp of soul that flickers and dies,
Have lightened and raised the sense that is dazed,
  The poor maimed heart and the earth-bound eyes.

But we faltered each at the edge of speech,
  And what might have been is hid from the wise—
For the better or worse, for the blessing or curse—
  Though I dream of you still with the deep
  burning eyes.

THE REAL AND THE UNREAL.

I HEAR men speak, and yet I fail
   The sense of their words to know ;
I see them pass as if through a veil,
   As they dimly come and go ;

But forms there are on either hand,
   And oh ! they are plain to see !
And each word that they speak I understand,
   When they tarry the day with me.

NOTE.—If I remember rightly, the late Mr. S. Moses once
wrote to this effect :—" I seem to live three lives."

A PAGE IN A CLOSE-SEALED BOOK.

I NEVER could read that sweet strange look,
  Or know what it meant to say ;
'Twas a page to me in a close-sealed book,—
  'Twill be to my dying day.

But much would I give, when that look you wore,—
  Could a human breast lie bare—
To have look'd right through to the heart's deep
    core,
  With its world that was imaged there.

THE FIRST TO CROSS.

PERHAPS, old friend, you'll be the first
　　To cross the narrow way ;
To learn what's there, the best or worst,
　　Whilst we still fighting stay.

Well, well, perhaps, same end, same war,
　　May be in that new land ;
And thou wilt bring thy help from far,
　　And in the old ranks stand.

"OH! WHAT HAVE YOU DONE?"

" Oh what have you done," my heart it cries,
"With the keen bright joyous face,
With the look of command, and the fearless eyes,
With the easy loving grace ?"

And a thrill of pain goes through my heart :—
" Were they lost by the world's rough wear,
Or bartered away at the great gold mart,
And tossed in the world's dust there?"

ONE MORE HEART-ACHE.

ONE more heart-ache, for the human race,—
So many have gone before,
It can hardly count in the great amount,—
Just one heart-ache the more!

One more heart-ache for you and for me,—
And some have gone before;
Oh! they come with the years, and they go with
the years,—
Just one heart-ache the more!

116

"WAS IT WORTH NO MORE?"

"Was love of mine not true enough,
  Was I not all to thee,
To laugh and to weep, to wake and to sleep,
  Just as thy mood might be ;

"And this fruit of the years, that had grown and
    grown,
  Was it worth no more than this,—
To cast it away in a single day,
  For the sake of your light love's kiss?"

THE TORCH-BEARERS.

SUCH they were who tried to know,
  Brave hearts fighting truly,
Through the darkness strove to go,
  Paid their stake so duly ;

Climbed, and found that yet there be
  Hills above them steeper ;
Held aloft a light, to see
  Darkness lying deeper.

THE VERY SAME STILL.

I know that one day I shall meet him,
   When walking there under the hill ;
I shall lift up my eyes and shall greet him,
   The same, and the very same still ;

The brow by its truth that was moulded,
   The eyes with their kindly play,
And the smile that was gently unfolded,
   Like the dawn of a summer day.

"ALONE WHERE THE GREAT SHIPS GO."

'Tis lightly she treads through heath and fern,
 And the sea-blown rock has won,
And late she stays through the dreaming days,
 And sings to the westering sun.

" Oh ! far out there my path shall be,
 Although the rough winds blow ;
Alone, in my boat I'll sail the sea,
 Alone, where the great ships go.

" My boat it shall be so staunch and true,
 Not wind, not wave, shall it fear ;
And the lonely night I'll trim my light,
 And watch for the dawn's good cheer.

"And through calm and storm, the sea and the sky
 Shall keep me as child of their own,
While the speeding ships come sailing by,
 And greet me, and leave me alone."

STAR COMRADES.

Oh ! you of the skies, and I of the earth,
  Through all the spaces that sever,
How often we've trodden the pilgrim's path,
  And taken sweet counsel together !

How often you soothed the pain and the strife,
  When wood and plain were sleeping,
And I gave you the hopes and the loves of a life
  To take in your tender keeping.

THE MEN WHO LEARN TO LIVE.

You'll carry the flag—the old torn rag—
  You'll carry the flag to the fore,
Through the press and the strain and the deadly
    rain,
  Where the fathers passed before.

And you'll stand by the flag, when the faint hearts
    fly,
  And the best that you have you'll give ;
For the men, who have learnt for a cause to die,
  Are the men who learn to live !

UNHELPED.

She has borne the boy in her arms with speed,
  Through the hours of day and night,
And it never failed in the time of need,—
  Her woman's strength so slight.

She has dug the grave where the trees gave
    space,
  And oh ! that minute sore,—
With the last vain look at the sweet proud face
And the smile that the lips still wore.

THE PLACE OF SLEEP.

IF I could choose, when comes the night,
  Where the last long sleep should be,
I'd choose the arrowy windy height,
  That parteth sea from sea.

For on all this earth there's never a place,
  Where the breezes blow so free,
Or the heaven has looked with such tender grace
  On wandering you and me.

"THY PRIDE IS GREAT."

"Oh ! child, thy pride is great, and yet
  I stand and say no more—
Thy breast against the world's edge set—
  Oh ! it shall hurt thee sore.

"And hast thou measured all the loss,—
  The pain, that waits for thee,
Cans't bear, till life's far end, the cross,
  That falls to-day on thee ? "

TO HAVE GUESSED AT THE RIDDLE.

GOOD-BYE, old world, for good and for ill,
  Oh ! much thou hast been to me ;
Thou hast filled the cup, and I've drunk it up,
  And I have no blame for thee.

Whatever thou art, a dream of the heart,
  Some story the brain invents,
Or a camping ground for the homeward bound,
  Who tarry a day in thy tents—

'Tis little I've read—whatever it mean—
  With this faltering brain of mine ;
But still, old world, it is good to have been,
  And guessed at this riddle of thine.

OH WHAT WOULD IT MATTER?

OH ! what would it matter to-night, love,
  If our two hearts should break,—
The earth would roll on all right, love,
  Nor trouble for our poor sake ;

The stars would look down from their giddy
      height,
  And the deep blue deeper grow,
Till the sun broke free from the clinging night,
  To waken his world below.

LOVING AS THE PEOPLE DO.

THERE we sat and took our pleasure,
  Ever old, yet ever new,
With the changing crowd around us,—
  Loving as the people do ;

Sat upon the benches watching
  Rich and poor their way pursue,
Wholly lost in one another,—
  Loving as the people do ;

Heard the hours of evening striking,
  Saw the idlers growing few,
Still we sat, and still we chatted,—
  Loving as the people do.

Then there came a time we parted,—
  Something crept between us two,
And no more we met and lingered,—
  Loving as the people do ;

Till again you went a-courting,—
  Was her heart as good and true ?—
And you sat again and chatted,—
  Loving as the people do ;

So the bitter tears rose upwards,
  As I passed and looked at you ;
Thus it fares with human loving,—
  Loving as the people do.

THE GOLDEN STORES THAT WANE.

THE blue dips down on every side,
   We walk together, I and you,
And mean to pierce, whate'er betide,
   Deeper and deeper in the blue.

Such joyous strength, such hours unspent,
   Oh ! can it be, old friend,
These golden stores of life are meant
   To wane and touch their end ?

A QUESTION IN ST. GEORGE'S CHURCH.

OH ! how will it be in twenty years—
　Will the gloss be faded and threads be bare,
Will scorn be born and weariness come—
　The love of to-day, that shews so fair ?

Or deeper and fuller, as life flows fast,
　With the passionate colours grown more fine,
With the dross burnt out in the trials past,
　And the pure gold left of the love divine ?

THE DEBT TO PAY.

" But leave me now and loose my hand,"
    He said, as he dying lay,
" For the evil spirits around me stand,
    And the debt is due to pay.

" They stay by me, the old-time deeds,
    That never undone can be ;
    Too late, too late, thy spirit pleads,—
    All help is vain for me."

A SMALL STRAY PART.

THOU great strong sea, fast-locked in dreams,
  Clouds journeying to and fro,
And tender blue the stars come through,—
  I can but love ye so !

Ye take possession of my heart,
  And all my life renew ;
Like grain of dust, I grow a part,
  A small stray part in you.

A FOREST SECRET.

OH ! there is a nook—if ye will not tell—
  Deep down in forest glade ;
And nowhere in the land doth dwell,
  A sunnier-hearted maid.

For oh ! she's blythe as bird on bush,
  That carols all day long ;
And morning light till dewy night,
  Her heart goes out in song.

VAINLY SET.

Go, weave your enchantments for others,
  Take all that you can in your net ;
May it bring you a host of new lovers,—
  For me it was vainly set ;

For the keen pale lips, and the delicate lines,
  That moved with the mouth's soft play,
And the eyes, that waited and watched, were
    signs,
  To scare away the prey ;

And I knew that the heart in its passionate way
  Was ready to love or hate,
To love its lover for half a day,
  Then send him back to his fate.

WAITING.

WHEN the dull wave leapt at the cliff, it died
    In an angry flash of white ;
And we know there is trouble far-off outside,—
    A trouble that comes with night ;

And we sit and listen, while storm-clouds fly,
    Till the low moan reaches the ear,
Which tells that the hounds of strife are in cry,
    And the hour of passion is here.

REST ON.

REST on, till peace thy heart shall steep,
  Thou dear thing tempest-tost ;
Thou hast waded through the waters deep,
  Where souls are well-nigh lost.

Rest on, and place thy hand in mine,
  Till peace shall come to thee,
And the sun once more in thy Heaven shall shine,
  And the great load lifted be.

THE GREAT WORLD-TIDE.

" There is never a word of blame from me,—
    You strove to be true to the past,
And the little hands clung where the frail weeds
        hung,
    When the world-tide swept so fast.

It wasn't your fault, my sweet little girl,
    But only the fault of the tide,
That has carried away with its mighty swirl
    So many a heart beside."

"DO YOU CALL THE LIVING THE DEAD?"

" THE dead ! Is it you, who call us the dead,—
  What you, who wait for the birth,
Who wait to pass hence from the prison of sense,
  From the body and brain of earth ?

Oh ! why do you name the living the dead,—
  Who think and who move with the force
Of the light, that from far, that from star unto
    star,
  Travels on in its tireless course ?"

AWAY FROM THE TRACK OF THE WORLD.

You came to my lonely shelter,
  So far from the track of the world,
Where the maddest of winds hold revel,
  And the wave on the rock is hurled.

You came, and there linger yet,
  In that haunt of the wild sea birds,
Sweet ghosts of your kindly glances,
  And joyous sunny words.

A LANGUAGE WITHOUT A KEY.

OF learning a store he has gathered and more,
  But his learning can't help him to-day ;
For to read is his part in the book of the heart,
  And spell, if he may, what its hieroglyphs say.

'Tis for him to divine what thing in that shrine
  Has moulded at will the sweet years of youth,—
Some imp of mere pelf, of fashion, and self,
  Or a dear little god of love and of truth.

And the innocent way, with its smile and love-play,
  Can't help, because smiles are so easy to wear ;
And a dress, as we know, though cut rather low,
  Has never as yet left any heart bare.

DREAMERS OF DREAMS.

Oh ! love, my love, but a moment so,
  Oh ! love, my love, but a moment more ;
And we'll cast from our thought what the sweet
    days brought,
  And we'll each return to what was before.

For dreamers of dreams we both have been,
  Never, oh ! never, the thing could be ;
For you is the peace of the bay within,
  And for me are the storms of the open sea.

HIS TIRED SMILE.

Oh ! bravely we christen the right and the wrong,
  To serve the needs of the day ;
The crookedest path that gains our end
  We declare to be God's way ;
And the great God smiles with his tired smile,
  As he hears what we mannikins say.

We know whatever the great God thinks,
  As well as himself, I trust,
So we gild the thing with holy words
  For which in our hearts we lust ;
And the great God smiles with his tired smile,
  As he watches us crawl in the dust.

" IF ONCE ——"

He had won it all—the name and fame,
All gifts that the world could give ;
But there comes at last the end of the game,
And he knew that he could not live.

He touched my hand as I stood at his side—
His meanest of friends was I—
" Oh ! if I had loved but once," he cried,
" 'Twere easy enough to die ! "

THE WANDERING RACE.

" In the pampered town for this weary while
  We've reeked and sweltered in dust and din,
  Where the mincing women are dolls who smile,
  With never a soul that feels within;

" And the trade of the men is the trade of words,
  To trick each other and trip if they can ;
  While their beards grow grey, and their life ebbs
        away,
  Ere ever they come to the strength of a man.

" Oh ! we'll not stay till it's time to die,
  But pass on our way and again be free,
  Where the great hills stand and speak with the sky,
  And the great plains roll with the joy of the sea ;

" And on, still on, through the wind and the sun,
  To share with the stars the watches of night,
Till the soul finds room for itself to be one
        With the sky and her children of gloom and
        light."

OUR TALK IN THE GARDEN-GROUND.

I think of our talk how it drifted,
　　As we walked in your garden-ground,
With the hem of your skirt just lifted,
　　To wade in some subject profound,—

How the socialist clubs were proposing
　　To manage the steeds of the sun ;
And the psychical folk were disclosing
　　A soul and a life to come ;

And you talked, on the marble rail leaning,
　　Till you cried " We're ready for tea";—
And the thing was as full of meaning,—
　　As a thing in fine life can be !

THE RIVAL WORLDS.

THE blue in the sky with an undimmed sun,
  The blue in the sea below,
Like sister souls, which grow into one ;—
  'Twill cost a pain to go.

Oh! fine—into sight when that new world breaks,—
  And yet perhaps when there,
I may wish to be back to the sins and the aches
  Of this world so tender fair.

THE JOY AND PAIN OF IT ALL.

WILL you ride and ride, when the sun is high,
 And the strong heat sickens the brain,
Will you lay you to sleep beneath the sky,
 When the dews fall cold on the plain ;

Will you keep the word like a faithful mate,
 That never it pass your lip ;
And the small steel thing,—will you hold it straight,
 And press with the finger-tip ;

Will you bear to look with a calm proud heart,
 As the best of the comrades fall ?—
Then, welcome, fair maid, to take your part
 In the joy and pain of it all.

THROUGH THE SMALL PANES.

THOUGH small the panes that I peer through,
  And grim the walls I see,
One fir that grows into the blue,
  Is good heart's feast for me ;

Though dank mists creep, like sorrows of old,
  And dim my picture o'er,
Yet the bright winds drive them back to their fold,
  And give me my sky once more.

A PLEA.

" IT was but a moment,—the hurt and the loss—
   For ever I loved you well ;
But how could I fight with the stars in their course,
   With their mad and their wanton spell ?

" For the stars they made from the earth's light dust
   A heart that should wander and stray,
That should love and forget as the stars rise and
      set,—
   The stars in their changeful play.

" They touched it with hues of leaping fire,
   With shadows and gleams from the sea,
With the flush of the dawn and its sweet desire,
   And a kiss of the wind so free.

" Yet all my life I have loved you well,
   As a child in its play loves child ;
But a heart, that the stars have bound by a spell,
   Must follow their fancies wild."

FAR AND FAINT.

THY sounds, oh storm, are far and faint,
  As thou stridest over the sea,
And we need thy breath from many a taint
  To set us clean and free.

But when thou comest on mighty wings,
  Deal gently with forest and tree,
For my heart is woe for the goodly things,
  That to-morrow will cease to be.

SHE OF THE SCORNFUL EYES.

She looked at all with level eyes,
  So fair, so proud, so calm,
As though she were a god who looked,
  And feared to take no harm.

From gifts of heart she turned away,—
  None brought the love she sought ;
She held in scorn the earthly clay,
  From which those hearts were wrought.

And yet, and yet, as years go on,
  Till their revenge is due,
Will dreams outlived grow cold and wan,
  Will clay grow warm and true ?

LOVE HATH NO PART.

Not love, poor child, but passion wild,
  That in thy heart is set ;
Love hath no part in thee, thy heart
  Has never loved as yet.

Oh ! there is much to cast away,
  And much through pain to earn,
And costly price for hearts to pay,
  'Ere love's deep truths they learn.

TRANSFORMATION.

Ah ! once was a maid in the far-off days,
  With eyes that drooped and with looks demure ;
And he who had watched her child-like ways,
  Of the soul within would have felt quite sure.

But the soul it is gone,—it has shrivelled away,
  And the child-like innocent looks have died ;
And there only remain the scheming brain,
  The viper's tongue, and the mask outside.

THE ROVING MEN.

Ye have tied me down to the desk and the pen,
  The hurrying pen all day,
But my heart is in the tents of the men,
  Who are roving far away.

I picture it all, and my blood is stirred,
  As by unknown lakes they go,—
The ring of the axe, and the leader's word,
  Where the stubborn forests grow.

Oh ! I'll not stay, or my heart will break,
  Tied down in this tame sheeps' pen,
For I thirst for the strife and the toiling life,
  In the tents of the roving men.

LIKE BIRDS BLOWN FAR AWAY.

THE sea and its waves are sleeping,
  And the houses gleam through the haze ;
And somewhere there you are keeping
  Your circle of happy days.

And I wonder if thoughts you don't utter,
  Like birds that are blown far away,
Down here on the rocks may flutter,
  Their moment or two to stay.

SO LIKE HELL.

Aʜ ! the crowd that streams around me,
  Endless through the weary street,
Beating out an iron music
  From the pavement at its feet.

Where the busy push and jostle,
  And the idle stare and stroll,
With their glances that can't mingle,
  And that only hurt the soul.

Ah that city ! with its passions,
  So like hell turned loose to play,
Rich and poor, before their idols,
  Giving life and soul away.

THE BRIDE WHO WAS FEY.

" Thou hast stolen my love with thy pretty face,
  And thy cheeks so pink to see ;
And he kissed you there at the very same place,
  That his kisses were given to me.

" Thou hast stolen my love with thy laugh so gay,
  But little the gain shall be—
From the bridal dress that thou wearest to-day,
  They shall fashion the shroud for thee."

A THIRD.

" Oh ! why are you grown so strange and chill,
   In days of loving but only three,
That no more in your arms you fold me still,
   But you stand, as in fear, away from me ? "

" I cannot fold you in arms of love,
   For there's something comes 'twixt me and you;
It is cold and white, and it clings all night,
   As lovers of old are fain to do."

THE SAIL IT FLAPPED.

THE sail it flapped as she slacked her course,
   And it flapped with an evil sound,
For the wind had dropped to gather its force,
   And already was veering round.

Then on it came, till the white lake hissed,
   At the touch of its short sharp breath,
And our words were few, for the game, we knew,
   Was a game of life and death.

And the good boat leant till she seemed to strike
   The water's face with her mast ;
And the mad waves rose like hidden foes,
   That seize on their prey at last.

But she shook them off and righted herself,
   In the teeth of the stress and the strain,
And we smiled, for we knew, if we steered her true,
   That the wind's wild rage was vain.

AT THE BALL.

Oh ! beautiful so, as I saw her then—
And beautiful so, as I see her still—
While the stars, that hold the scales for men,
  Were weighing for us the good and the ill.

And I touched her hand—but down the stair
  Came the sweet dream notes, and spoilt the
    charm,
And I only said, though she looked so fair—
  " Will you dance once more ; will you take my
    —arm ?"

THY KISS ENCLOSES.

Kiss me love, and let me live,
  Live and draw from love's full store;
Kiss me love,—and let me die,
  Praying, craving, nothing more.

Kiss me love, thy kiss encloses
  All sweet things and makes them mine,—
Dews of heaven, and scent of roses,
  Song of birds, and rich sunshine.

WITH FAINT STARS THINLY SOWN.

I look into that tender blue,
  With faint stars thinly sown ;
I travel on through great plains new,
  Yet do not feel alone.

That tender blue,—I watch and stand,
  And I am safe, I know ;
It arches down on either hand,
  And holds me as I go.

WITHOUT YOUR HAND.

" I cried in vain—' I was too weak,
    Too weak to stand alone '—
Some natures are by passing breath,
    So lightly overthrown.

" Ah ! cruel in your strength to think,
    That I like you was strong ;
Without your hand I fail to stand,
    And yield to bitter wrong."

THINGS FAR APART.

" THE fault of the past—does it last and last ?—
Now tell me, tell me true,—
Is the love that we had for each other on earth,—
Is it counted a sin for you ? "

" Whatever I loved with loyal heart,
Oh ! that is a gain to me ;
But the true and the false are far apart,
In all the worlds that be."

SHALL SIN NO MORE.

" Oh ! turn again, but once again,—
　　These lips shall sin no more ;
　　These lips, with words like cruel swords,
　　Which hurt thy heart so sore.

" I'll seal them with a double seal,
　　That they shall sin no more ;
　　I'll love thee so that thou shalt feel
　　I never loved before."

THE HOUR OF WONDER.

THE great strong hills their vantage keep,
　But their pride shall be humbled to-night,
And our foot shall be set on the peak that holds
　The last of the evening light.

And when we have climbed and climbed we will
　　sleep,
　Or talk the hours away,
In the silver light of the sweet June night,
　Which is but a dream of the day ;

Till there comes, like a god, to the waiting hill,
　The first rose-flush from above,
And the soul that watches is hushed and still,
　In that hour of wonder and love.

THE ANSWER.

THEN let thine answer be confest,—
If thou shouldst answer " yea,"
Oh ! wear two roses at thy breast,
Two loves, two lives, to say.

But if thy heart should answer " nay,"
No rose then shalt thou wear,—
No blood-red gracious rose to say,
Love finds its sweet home there.

TOO FINE FOR EYES TO SEE.

Aye ! nothing, less than nothing,
  Could each to the other be ;
Yet gossamer threads were woven,
  Too fine for eyes to see ;

Such threads as stretch through darkness,
  Through time and far off space,
And keep two lives still touching,
  When face is lost to face.

ON TRAMP.

OH! place your hand, my lass, in mine,
　And off and away we'll go,
For little we care what serves for fare,
　Or makes the bed below.

And we never are sad as we journey along,
　Though smile or frown the day,
For the worst of our luck we turn to a song,
　In our careless tramping way.

THE WAY NO LOVERS KNEW.

Oh ! let us love, sweet heart, so true,
  Till hearts can love no more,—
Till men shall say no lovers knew,
  The way to love before.

And when it's all worn out and done,
  And these few years are o'er,
We'll find some world beyond the sun,
  Where hearts can still love more.

BACK TO THE WORLD.

GOODBYE—the hour its summons brings,—
   Those moments few at end,
In which you talked of strange new things
   With your chance wandering friend !

And now the world's swift rushing stream
   Has caught you, sweeps you back,
From where we strayed by paths of dream
   Beyond life's daily track.

THE WONDER-WORLD OUTSIDE.

"Oh ! let me come and sit by thee,
  For thou hast known and tried,
And tell me what it holds for me—
  That wonder-world outside.

"Oh ! will their talk range far and bold,
  Like flight of bird in sky,
And pass o'er worlds, the new, the old,
  While soul to soul draws nigh.

"And shall we ever strive to know,
  And turn from feast and rest ;
And will sweet talk still flow and flow,
  While suns dip in the west ?

"Will deeds to do, the pulses stir,—
  To save a race undone ;
Till some low whisper fills the ear :—
  'Shall we two fight as one ? '"

BLURRED EDGES.

THEY are round me to-night in the gloaming,
  Their voices fall on my ear ;
They seem to hover and touch me,
  But I like them and have no fear.

And where one world beginneth,
  And where the other is done,
I cannot tell, for the edges
  Are blurred and mixed in one.

IN THE YEARS AFTER THE SALE.

She sits at her glass with musing heart,
And thinks of the days that were,
Before she sold at the world's great mart
That face so passing fair.

And she wonders what she would give and give,
If out of that glass could rise
A face that lies dead in the years that are fled,
With the hope and the trust in its eyes.

BACK TO THE SEA-MOTHER.

KINDEST of mothers, from whom I have strayed,
　Back again tired I come to thee,
Chanting and crooning the old wave-song,—
　Sing it, oh ! sing it again to me !

Weary and spent, as the hour draws near,—
　Hush me to sleep with that soft wave-song ;
Wash all the cares away, wash all the strifes away,
　All the old pains that to living belong.

Down at thy side I place me to rest ;
　Slowly my senses are stealing from me ;
Passions and pleadings have ceased in my breast ;
　Gently my spirit floats away free.

ONE BREATHLESS MOMENT.

THE race was for life and death when we met—
One breathless moment to speak—
And my hand against her breast she set,
And her lips just touched my cheek.

Then the world grew mine, and was filled with
delight,
As rare and rich could be ;
Till on she passed and was lost in the night,
And all was a dream to me.

THOU HAST WON THE RIGHT.

OH ! my brave one, thou hast carried
   Heart of steel and heart of gold ;
Now thy road is sloping downward,
   Now the days are nearly told.

Thou hast fought thy fight so truly,
   Never flinched from face of foe,
Faultless courage, ceaseless loving,—
   Thou hast won the right to go.

ONE WHO HAD TRAVELLED FAR.

As she entered the room, she claimed your heart,—
  Her beauty so finely she wore ;   .
And you felt that to love her was just your part,
  With the hope of nothing more.

So I left my heart in the dust at her feet,
  And I sailed across the sea,
For I said to myself, perchance we should meet,
  When the better time might be.

And I saw her again—strange dreams there are—
  So weary and wan to see,
With the look of one who had travelled far,—
  From another world, may be.

HUSKS.

Ah ! the craving that fills the heart,
　Sense of emptiness, sense of loss,
Never from touch of the world apart,
　Changing the handfuls of dross for dross.

Ah ! to live the shadows among,
　Miss the touch of the infinite whole,
Never to win to the heart within,
　Never be one with nature's soul.

SQUIRE MUDGE IN SUNSHINE.

OLD Squire Mudge is happy to day,
   And he whistles a stave as he goes to his gate,
For the rain has come down on his neighbour's
      hay—
   " That old fool Jenkins, who's always late."

And Farmer Cox has his men on strike,
   And they've left the hay and have lost their pay,
And rumour is rife that Sir Anthony's wife
   From her lawful lord has tripped away.

And the Smiths have a daughter instead of a son,
   And Lord F. is in debt and must let the old hall ;
And the world on the whole makes capital fun,
   When Providence chastens our neighbours all !

181

A WIND TO CROSS THE SEA.

" Oh ! how shall I know if your heart be stirred
  By a love that is not for me ;
 Is there ever a wind to bring me word,
  Across the far far sea ? "

" Oh ! nothing I know of the winds of the sea,
  But love and life are one ;
 And whenever this heart thinks not of thee,
  It's thinking will be done."

A LESSON IN PHILOSOPHY.

THE summer was hot, and the flies were sore ;
They snatched at the food, and swarmed in the face,
Till my patience at last was destroyed, and I swore
That such vile little wretches had no claims for
grace.

But philosophy presently softened my speech :—
" Poor things," I exclaimed, " I will wish you
no harm ;
For Providence means you a lesson to teach,—
In the midst of our worries to keep the soul calm.

" Some good folk I know,—they are just of your
kind ;
They are gifted like you with a scent for their
game ;
And they gather and feed on whatever they find,—
Be it sweetmeat or carrion,—it serves just the
same."

AND YET—GOOD-BYE.

"The right and the wrong, the weal and the woe—
Thy word shall turn the scale ;
Shall we loose our hands and let them go ;
Or hold, till all things fail ? "

" Oh ! right and wrong are but words of a song,
And the life beyond but a lie,
And you are my all in this one real world,
And yet—and yet—good-bye."

THRICE AGAIN.

" I TURNED from my friends, and I left my home—
    The ties were sore to break—
And the creed in my heart that was planted
    there,
    I tore it up for your sake.

" But what did it count? I would do it again ;
    And thrice again for you,—
If the clay could stir, if the dead could hear,
    And care what thing 1 do."

OH! HOW WILL IT BE?

" To ride with me o'er yonder plain,
　　Fair maid, is that your mind,
　　Cross rivers and hills, and never draw rein,
　　But leave old worlds behind?"

" And when the rivers and hills are cros't,
　　Oh! how will it be with me,
　　If your heart to another maid be lost,
　　And you let the old love be?"

A LAST WORD.

" THERE'S summut I'd like you chaps to tell—
　　There's a minute or two, mebbe—
If yer has a heart that loves yer well,—
　　Don't throw it away from ye.

"The rest of the things yer may chuck as yer
　　choose,—
　　There's none of 'em vallies a pin ;
But a heart that loves, yer should nivver lose,—
　　Yer may nivver git it agin."

BETTER IT SO SHOULD BE.

THROUGH the plain and the wood we will wander
apart,
And apart will sail the sea,
And no more will I speak from an open heart,
Or journey the day with thee ;

And we'll never hold hands in the coming time,
For it's only a grief to me ;
And the higher the hills between us climb—
Oh ! better it so should be !

SINKING WITH YOU.

" So I, fair sir, your soul must redeem,
  And your guardian angel grow,
And bear you up in the fierce mid-stream,
  Where the great tides come and go.

" But how would it be, if the past were a past
  That no human heart could undo,
And my strength should fail, and I found at
    the last
  That I could but sink with you ? "

THERE CAME A SMILE.

As if to the earth, so low he bowed—
    " I go my way ",—cried he ;
And she curtsied deep, and she curtsied proud—
    " Too much of grace for me."

Three steps on their way, and they pause awhile,
    And each looked back just then ;
When through the tears there came a smile,
    And made them one again.

SUMMARY JUSTICE.

He clenched his hand, he stamped his foot,—
Bright flushed the little cheek :—
" If I were King, I'd do this thing—
Cut heads off every week.

" Oh ! in my realm bad men no more
Should live by land or sea ;
And in all hearts,—I'd make a law,—
No wicked thoughts should be ! "

AND THE TRUE LOVE WAITS.

" THEN ride not in the vale at night,
    For an evil thing is there ;
And if thou meetest the maid in white,
    So close thine eyes in prayer."

" Oh ! I'll not stay for fiend or flood,
    But through the night I'll ride,
For my true love of flesh and blood
    Dwells there on the further side."

    *   *   *   *   *

She stands in his path, so near, so clear,
    Although the moonlight dies,—
" Now stay, fair sir, if thou hast no fear
    To look in a maiden's eyes."

So long, so deep, she looks in his eyes,
    Till over him comes the sleep ;
And the true love waits, while the love-time
    flies,—
    Will wait and wait and weep.

THE UNKNOWN SHORE.

It falls on my ear, now faint, now strong,
  The thunderous note of the distant roar,
The surf of the sea I have sailed so long,
  As it beats at last on the unknown shore.

Oh ! how will it be, when the hour has come,—
  Unlike all hours that went before,—
Will help be near, or in pain and fear,
  Shall I win my way to the unknown shore ?

IN BORDERLAND.

FOR strange deep longings move us,
  As betwixt the two we stand,
And share in the mystic meetings
  And partings in borderland ;

When day and night so gently
  Touch hands, and fall apart,
Like those in life forbidden,
  Heart should be one with heart.